This picture book helps children learn about mathematical concepts through a colorful and entertaining story.

Math concepts explored may include:
• Understanding math concepts
• Patterns and problem solving
• Introducing mathematical concepts that are found in our surroundings to give children a fresh perspective on math: math in art

About the Authors
Majoongmul is a Korean word that refers to "priming water" poured into a pump to start the flow before pumping water from a well. **Group Majoongmul** is the name of the authors' group that creates books that serve as the priming water within children's hearts.

About the Illustrator
Yun-ju Kim majored in industrial arts in college and studied illustration in London. She enjoys creating illustrations while teaching at the university level.

Tan Tan Math Story ***Math at the Art Museum***

Original Korean edition © Yeowon Media Co., Ltd

This U.S edition published in 2015 by TANTAN PUBLISHING INC, 4005 W Olympic Blvd, Los Angeles, CA 90019-3258

U.S and Canada Edition © TANTAN PUBLISHING INC in 2015

ISBN: 978-939248-03-9

Printed in South Korea at Choil Munhwa Printing Co., 12 Seongsuiro 20 gil, Seongdong-gu, Seoul.

Math at
the Art Museum

Written by Group Majoongmul

Illustrated by Yun-ju Kim

✿TanTan Publishing

My sister and I are going to the art museum with our parents! "It's interesting that math can be found in art," Dad says.

"Math in art? Is that even possible?" I ask.

"Come—let's find out," he replies.

A big poster in front of the museum reads:
DISCOVER MATH IN ART.

We hurry into the museum.

**DISCOVER
MATH IN ART**

Art Museum
February 1 to March 1

"The subject of this painting is numerals," Dad says.

Mom leads us to another painting. "The artist used many dots of paint to show people in a park on a sunny afternoon," she says. "It took a lot of work, but the painting is beautiful!"

Georges Seurat, *A Sunday Afternoon on the Island of La Grande Jatte*

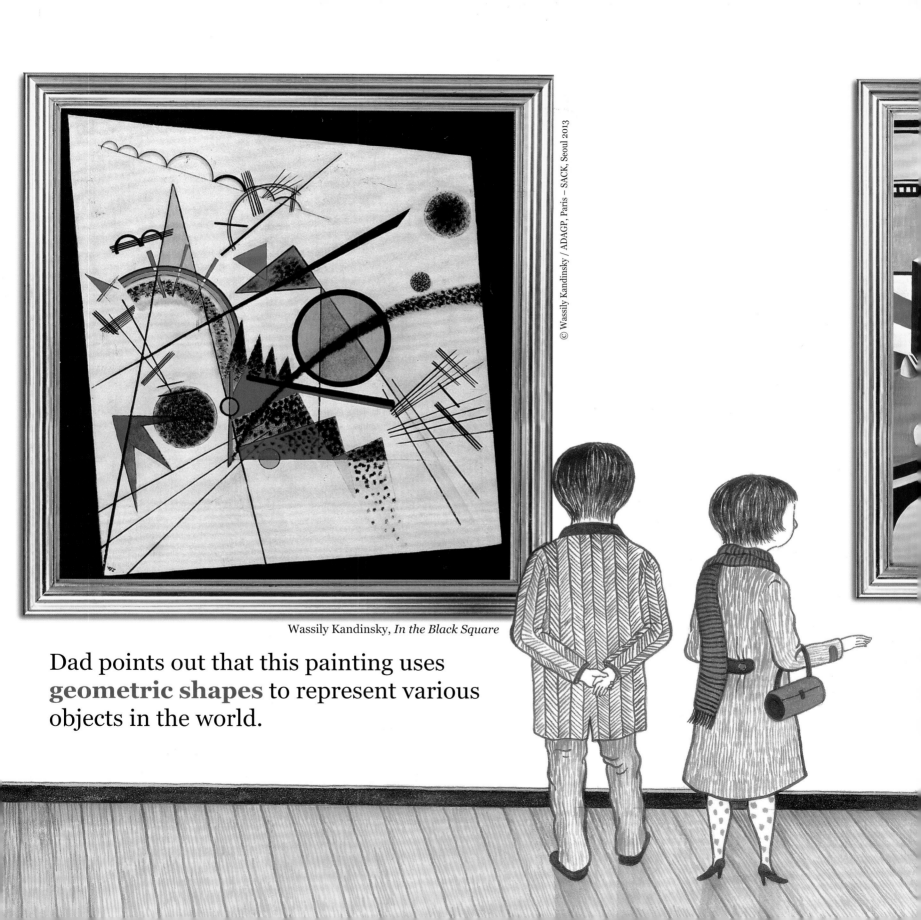

Wassily Kandinsky, *In the Black Square*

Dad points out that this painting uses **geometric shapes** to represent various objects in the world.

"Aha!" says Dad. "In this one, the painter used **geometric shapes** to represent mechanical parts."

Fernand Léger, *Mechanical Elements*

Some artists use **spheres** to represent faces and **cylinders** for arms and legs. What three-dimensional shapes might be used as parts of the human body?

Pablo Picasso, *Marie-Thérèse*

Dad says the face in this painting is strange!
The painting shows two views of the face—from
the front and from the side—joined together.

Some artists, including Picasso, composed their paintings as though they were looking at an object from different **directions** and **angles**. They believed the subject could be expressed more fully that way.

Edgar Degas, *Miss La La at the Cirque Fernando*

This painting of an acrobat has the perspective of **looking up from below**.

Edgar Degas, *The Star*

This pastel work has the perspective of **looking down** from above. Viewed from a new perspective, a familiar object can look very different.

René Magritte, *The Promenades of Euclid*

The two **cones** have the same shape, but one becomes the roof of a building and the other is a long road in the paintings.

Meindert Hobbema, *The Alley at Middleharnis*

A sense of **distance** and **depth** can be created on flat paper by drawing smaller and fainter for distant objects and larger and sharper for closer objects.

Kim Jae-hong, *Praying Mother and Son Rock Formation*

"The symmetry reflected in the water is marvelous in this one!" Mom says.

Symmetry is when one shape becomes exactly like another if you flip, slide or turn it. The simplest type of Symmetry is Reflection or Mirror Symmetry.

Henri Matisse, *Large Composition with Masks*

"Ah, the artist has arranged **colors** and **shapes** so neatly," Dad says. "The collage is both beautiful and balanced."

Giuseppe Arcimboldo, *Four Seasons—Spring*

Giuseppe Arcimboldo, *Four Seasons—Summer*

Giuseppe Arcimboldo, *Four Seasons—Autumn*

Giuseppe Arcimboldo, *Four Seasons—Winter*

These paintings show how **parts** can become a **whole.** Various fruits, leaves, and other items are cleverly put together to create human faces.

Salvador Dali, *The Persistence of Memory*

Time is the subject of this painting. The past is the time that has already gone by. The present is the time we are in at any moment. The future is the time that is yet to come.

Salvador Dali's painting *The Persistence of Memory* sparks curiosity about the notion of time. Understanding the passage of time can help children develop skills to measure time divisions and units, which are essential mathematical concepts.

Dad says that a mathematician and architect named Leon Battista Alberti believed it is not possible to understand art without understanding and using mathematics.

That makes sense to me. Looking for math in paintings and other artwork is eye-opening!

Mathematical Elements in a Work of Art

This book highlights works of art that incorporate mathematical elements and principles. Although it may seem to some people that art and mathematics are entirely separate areas of focus, they are in fact closely related. Works of art use various math concepts, including the laws of perspective, symmetry, composition, the golden ratio, points, lines, and sides, among others. Over the years, developments in art and advancements in math have influenced each other. For example, although German mathematician August Ferdinand Möbius invented the Möbius strip, the one-sided surface also became an important subject for works of art in various media. *The Promenades of Euclid* is a painting about Greek mathematician Euclid and his geometric theories. In addition, South Korean illustrator Kim Jae-Hong's *Praying Mother and Son Rock Formation* showcases mathematical symmetry.

This book is not intended to analyze art from a mathematical perspective. Instead, the intent is to highlight how math often informs art and also influences our daily lives. Because math is not a field that deals only with numbers and calculations, it's important to encourage children to look for and learn from mathematical concepts in unexpected places, including in artwork.

Understanding Mathematical Concepts Used in Artworks

Drawing Mathematical Art

| **Activity Goal** | To make a work of art using various mathematical elements

| **Materials** | Colored pencils, glue, scissors, 4 index cards, colored paper of different sizes, and 4 sheets of large drawing paper for each player in the exercise

1 First, use one of the four index cards to write each word: *dots, lines, shapes*, and *number*. Turn all the cards over to hide the words. The child and the parent both receive a set of 4 large sheets of drawing paper and the colored paper.

2 Choose who goes first. The first player chooses an index card and must draw what is written on it. If the player picks the *shapes* card, he/she must draw different types of shapes on the drawing paper. For example, he/she might draw a picture that incorporates circles, triangles, and rectangles. The next player chooses a card and uses the word cue to inspire his/her drawing. Repeat these steps until all 4 cards have been used.

3 Players can then use the colored pencils to color their drawings, or they can cut out and and paste bits of colored paper onto their drawings to add more detail.

4 After each of the *dots, lines, shapes*, and *number* index cards has been used and four different pictures have been made by each player, give each of the works an interesting title and hang them all in a family art gallery.

5 Encourage all family members to discuss which mathematical elements are incorporated within each picture.

This is a drawing of the human body by Leonardo da Vinci, a famous Italian artist, mathematician, and inventor. Is your height greater than the length of your outstretched arms, from the end of one hand to the end of the other? The length of your outstretched arms is the same as your height!

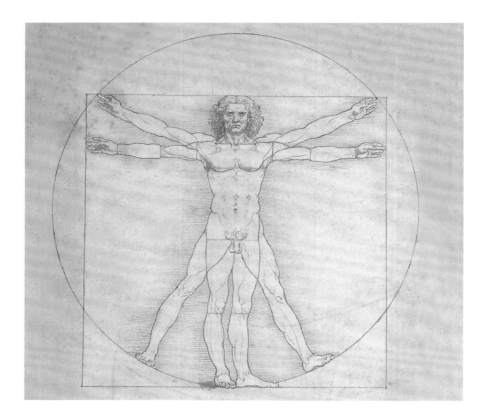

Have a friend lie on the floor with arms and legs outstretched as in Leonardo's drawing. Measure his/her height and arm span. Then have your friend spread his/her feet apart about a quarter of his/her height and raise his/her arms up as in the drawing. Use chalk to draw a circle around your friend's body. The center of the circle is his/her belly button, and his/her legs form an isosceles triangle (a triangle that has two sides of equal length). The proportions of the human body are fascinating!

The ratio that people feel is most peaceful and stable within objects is called the golden ratio, or the golden section.

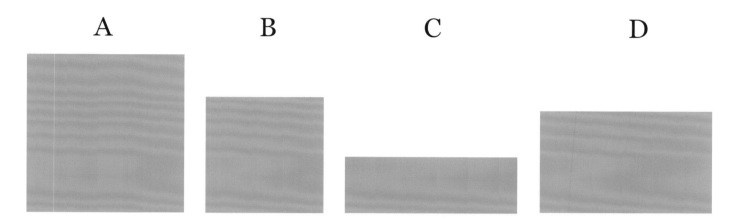

A   B   C   D

From the rectangles above, pick the one you like the most.
Which rectangle did you choose? Most people choose rectangle
D. The sides of rectangle D have the golden ratio.

The golden ratio was used in designing many architectural structures, including Egyptian pyramids and the Parthenon. It was also used in works of art by Leonardo da Vinci and Michelangelo. The golden ratio has even been used to determine the size of business cards and credit cards!

Max Bill, *Endless Ribbon*

The Surface with Only One Side

Max Bill used the concept of the Möbius strip as his theme for this sculpture. The one-sided endless strip was invented by mathematician August Ferdinand Möbius. The ends of Bill Max's flat piece of metal were twisted and joined to create the one-sided, endless shape.

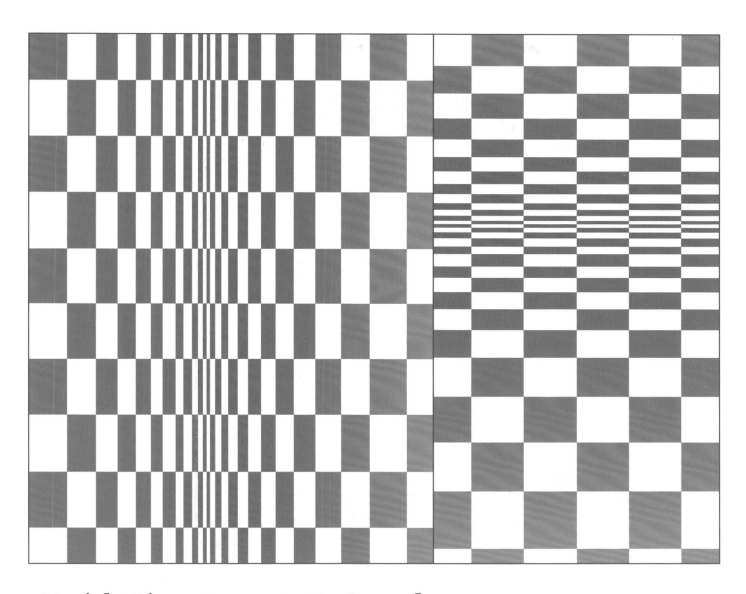

Straight Lines Appear to Be Curved

This drawing is made solely of rectangles, which have straight sides. However, an optical illusion makes it appear as though the drawing has curved lines and areas that seem to be moving. In addition to incorporating various mathematical concepts, some works of art create optical illusions.